Fabio
Villanueva

SPRING FEVER!

4th grade writing!

Other Apple Paperbacks
you will enjoy:

Bug Off!
by Terri Fields

Dead Meat!
by Moya Simons

Dirty Socks Don't Win Games
by Dean Marney

Help! I'm Trapped in My Teacher's Body
by Todd Strasser

Never Hit a Ghost with a Baseball Bat
by Eth Clifford

SPRING FEVER!

Peter Lerangis

AN
APPLE
PAPERBACK

SCHOLASTIC INC.
New York Toronto London Auckland Sydney

ISBN 0-590-25471-5

Copyright © 1995 by Peter Lerangis.
All rights reserved. Published by Scholastic Inc.
APPLE PAPERBACKS is a registered trademark of Scholastic Inc.

12 11 10 9 8 7 6 5 4 3 2 1   5 6 7 8 9/9 0/0

Printed in the U.S.A.   40

First Scholastic printing, March 1995

For my mother,
Mary Condos Lerangis,
who gave me the greatest possible gifts:
a sense of humor,
a sense of purpose,
and most of all, love.

SPRING FEVER!

Prologue

I live in Hopnoodle Village.

I know, I know. I should feel lucky for growing up in such a famous place. And I guess I do.

Not everyone's village makes the TV news twelve nights in a row. You may have even seen me, the day the reporter was at the school interviewing students. (It's okay if you didn't, because I was picking my nose.) And you've heard all the reports about how great *Olde* Hopnoodle was, years ago.

But don't get the wrong impression. Between ancient times and the present, Hopnoodle was not famous at all. Far from it.

Actually, before the geeks arrived, it was kind of a dump.

By now you probably think you know everything about the geeks. But the story that made the news was the official grown-up version. No one has told the full, inside truth, from a *kid's* point of view.

Until now.

But I'm getting ahead of myself.

My name is Shawn Ferguson. Technically I'm Shawn Ferguson IV. (You can see the "IV" under some Wite-Out on my birth certificate. My mom had to do that because the maternity nurses thought it meant I needed intravenous feeding.) Now I'm in seventh grade. Like most of the Fergusons before me, I have reddish-brownish hair, smallish eyes, and flattish feet that point out too much.

My family has lived in Hopnoodle Village for four generations. My great-grandfather, Shawn Ferguson the first, moved here from Germany because he'd heard the streets of Hopnoodle were paved with gold. (They were, but it was just paint. During the first nasty winter, the plows scraped it all off the cobblestones.)

Shawn the first helped make Olde Hopnoodle great. Last fall, my dad and I found this sign when we were cleaning out our attic:

NOTHING SAYS "OOGA" LIKE A
HOPNOODLE HORN!

FOR MAXIMUM VOLUME,
LUXURIOUS SQUEEZABILITY,
AND THAT OH-SO-PERFECT TONE,
REMEMBER: DON'T BLOW IT . . .
UNLESS YOU HAVE A HOPNOODLE IN
YOUR CAR!

That's right. Years ago no one heard the sound "Ah-*OO*-gah!" without thinking: Hopnoodle.

Dad says that dozens of tourists used to flock to the Hopnoodle Ooga Horn factory every week. (Usually they wandered in by mistake, thinking it was the Flugschwester Hotel, which is next door. Still, the place was always jumping.)

But those glory days are over. Cars stopped using oogas long ago, and years later comedians did, too.

Last year the factory closed for good. The village really went downhill. It was no longer such an honor to say, "I am a Hopnoodlian." *I* sure stopped saying it.

People began moving out in droves. Dad, who was the factory foreman and president of Squeezers and Honkers Local 53, lost his job.

What was worse, the town next to us, Pifflethorn, started this huge information resources systems technology management business. I have no idea what that means, and neither does anyone else, but the kids there are super rich. And they never stop rubbing it in your face. Especially when it's your turn to be in the Skool-2-Skool exchange program, where a Hopnoodle student spends a week at Pifflethorn Middle School, and vice versa.

That happened to me once. It was pure torture. I'd call it about rock bottom in my life.

But I guess it's a perfect place to begin my story.

1

My Last Day at Pifflethorn

"**I**n conclusion," I read, "many scientists have begun to take seriously the idea that alien life may exist in some hospitable atmosphere — "

Bllllaaaaaaat!

The odor seeped toward me even before Sarah Blubstein shot out of her seat and screamed, "Buford far — "

"That's enough!" Mrs. Wigshaft interrupted. "Continue, Shawn."

Continue? I was gagging. My hair was starting to curl. All I wanted to do was bolt out of there. I tried to move backward to find a pocket of fresh air, but I was smack in front of Mrs. Wigshaft's desk.

Buford Tutweiler was sitting in the back row,

laughing his head off. All around him, kids were groaning and fanning the air with spiral notebooks.

I took a deep breath and almost passed out. But I valiantly kept reading: ". . . um, atmosphere in some other galaxy. Recent reports of unidentified flying objects — "

A plastic Slime Slug landed on my report.

I glanced up. Half the kids in the class looked about ready to explode with laughter (or lack of oxygen).

Behind me, Mrs. Wigshaft cleared her throat. "I fail to see the humor in all of this," she said.

Calmly, with great dignity, I brushed off the disgusting thing and continued: " — have been examined at the top levels of government . . ."

Dooo-weeeeee, doo doo doo doo doooooo. . . .

Now Ben Wheeler was singing the *Star Trek* theme, way out of tune. I shot him a Look. A Hard Look. The one that reduces my little brother to helpless tears.

He sang louder.

"Mr. *Wheeler*!" Mrs. Wigshaft yelled. "Will you let him finish?"

That was when I spotted Buford digging around in one of his nostrils. And grinning wickedly.

I was trapped. I turned to look at Mrs. Wigshaft, but now her face was buried in some papers.

"Go ahead, Shawn," she said without looking up.

"Ewwwwww," came Sarah's voice.

Quickly I turned back around. Buford had reached pay dirt. He was preparing his missile. Watching him, Sarah was turning green.

I raced through the last sentence. "And-I-for-one-look-forward-to-the-day-when-we-on-Earth-can-be-friends-with-an-extraterrestrial-race."

Too late.

Buford snapped his wrist. His booger hurtled toward me like a comet. The class had fallen silent and was watching the trajectory in awe.

What did I do? The only thing I could do. I ducked.

I hadn't stopped to think about Mrs. Wigshaft.

"*Aaaauughh!*" she cried. "What — who — ?"

When I turned toward her, she was frantically pawing at her hair.

The class was *gone*. Over the top. Left and right, bodies were convulsing onto the tile floor.

"Mr. Ferguson!" Mrs. Wigshaft screamed. "Was that your idea of a funny trick? Is this what *Hopnoodle* kids do for cheap laughs?"

"But I — I didn't — "

"*Yeeeee-hah-ha-ha-ha-ha!*" The laughter was so loud I couldn't hear myself stammering.

"Silence!" Mrs. Wigshaft smacked her palm on the desk top. "Shawn, sit down, please."

I slunk back to my desk. Good thing I looked before I sat.

The least Buford could have done was kill the poor bug before putting it on my seat. But it was alive, on its back, waggling its legs at me. Pleading for me not to squash it. For one last chance at life.

Or maybe it was just in shock from Buford's nuclear blast.

"DID YOU HEAR ME, YOUNG MAN!"

I quickly brushed the bug away. It flew onto Sarah Blubstein's lap.

I don't need to tell you how she reacted. I'll just say it took about three months for me to regain full hearing in my right ear.

What a rotten day.

Over and over, I said to myself, *It's my last day here*.

I never thought I'd look forward so much to returning to Hopnoodle Junior High. The Skool-2-Skool program was a real disaster. (Why was it called Skool-2-Skool? Great way to teach spelling, huh? My dad explained that the program was funded by a corporation, and corporations think they have to spell things wrong for good business. Hey, don't ask me.)

Anyway, I hadn't learned a thing, except that

the kids at Pifflethorn Middle School had it great compared to us.

Take the bathrooms. The Pifflethorn boys' rooms had climate control, posters on the walls, and toilets that flushed automatically when you walked away. (At Hopnoodle we didn't even have paper towels because the custodial budget ran out.) And their cafeteria? It was more like a four-star restaurant. You could have bacon-cheese-burgers every day if you wanted — or the specials, which were always things like Cajun chicken, pineapple pizza, and pasta with pesto (which is green and lumpy but tastes good).

But the main difference was the classes. The Pifflethorn kids could take cool subjects if they wanted, like Video Technology and Robot Design. I sat in on a Film Study class taught by this French dude who showed nothing but Jerry Lewis movies.

What a school.

Years ago, Skool-2-Skool kids actually had to do homework and keep up in class. But Pifflethorn's curriculum became a lot harder than Hopnoodle's, so now you only have to give a report on the "topic of your choice."

Which, for me, was extraterrestrials. Did I believe in them? Well, sort of. I'd never *seen* any.

And I doubt all those reports about alien abductions. But still, how can you not wonder?

Sometimes at night I just stare and stare at the sky. I try to focus on every single star. Have you done that? Your eyes start to glaze after a while. And of course, you've only seen, like, a trillionth of a zillionth of all the stars out there. And if you figure that each of them may have a whole solar system of planets . . . well, are we earthlings the *only* form of life among *all that*? I don't think so.

Stargazing had become kind of a hobby of mine. My dad's new job was driving a hot dog truck with a sunroof, and sometimes he let me ride with him to the depot after his late rounds.

For Dad, that job was kind of a comedown. He had been pretty high up in the squeezer/honker trade before it went bust. And, to be frank, his uniform was a little embarrassing. A rubber hot dog was attached to the top of his hat, and it wobbled whenever he moved his head. Plus, his jacket sleeves were shaped like hot dogs, too.

But Dad was cool about it. A job was a job.

And besides, the sunroof was great.

"Ahem . . . thank you, Shawn," Mrs. Wigshaft said coldly as she pulled her hair back into a ponytail. "That was an . . . illuminating report."

The class had calmed down. Sarah was red-faced but quiet. Buford was involved in his usual late-class activity, watching the clock.

"Well, Shawn, I hope you have benefited from your week at Pifflethorn," Mrs. Wigshaft went on. "And in continuing with our longstanding intrascholastic tradition, we will be sending to Hopnoodle a student of our own. . . ."

The second hand on the wall clock was inching upward. In nine seconds the school day would be over. And so would my week of torture.

Buford had already slid his butt off his seat. He was poised to be the first out the door.

"Beginning Monday, I hope your classmates at Hopnoodle will give a warm welcome to . . ."

Three seconds. I could smell freedom and it was sweet.

". . . Buford Tutweiler."

BRRRRIIINNNNNG!

Buford stood up suddenly. His thigh caught the edge of his desk and it toppled over.

My heart sank so fast, it made my stomach hurt. I was going to have to live with this guy another *week*?

Buford picked up his desk. Then he turned toward me, slowly. I tried to avoid his gaze as I gathered up my books.

"Heyyyy, Ferguson," he said with a cheesy

grin. "Looks like you and I are meant to be together."

"Yeah, right," I replied, hurrying out of the room.

The moment I was in the hallway, Buford's arm landed like a sack of oats on my shoulder. "What's the rush, dude?" he asked.

"Uh, Buford, you hate me," I reminded him. "Which is cool. I don't mind. So why don't we just, like, go our own separate ways — "

Buford looked offended. "Whoa, can I at least have the privilege of walking out with you?"

"Sure," I said with a weary sigh.

Buford had tried this once before. When we had reached the front of the school, he'd let out a huge burp, then pretended I had done it. (*Real* mature.)

I prepared myself for the worst.

As we walked outside, I heard a familiar sound: *Ah-OO-gah-OO-gah!*

Only one vehicle I know of has an old Hopnoodle Ooga Horn. I suddenly wanted to go back into the school. "Uh, Buford, I think I forgot — "

Buford was now standing near a huge pack of kids. "*Hey, Shawn!*" he called out in this exaggerated loud voice. "*Isn't that your dad in the Weiner's Wieners outfit?*"

A hundred Pifflethorn faces looked my way, then out to the curb.

There, beside the big white truck, with his rubber hot dog hat flapping in the breeze, was my dad. He grinned and waved at me.

"Weiner's Wieners! Red hot!" he shouted cheerfully. "Hi, son!"

I can still hear the laughter of those kids, just thinking about it.

I almost died.

2

Food Fight

I didn't miss Pifflethorn Middle School one bit on Monday. Until lunchtime, that is. *Then* I had second thoughts. The Hopnoodle cafeteria smell almost knocked me out.

My best friend, Adam Fenster, didn't seem to mind. He was trying to fix me up with a ninth-grade girl.

"Shawn, you are a total dork when it comes to girls," Adam said, as we pushed our trays down the lunch line.

"Great, say it a little louder," I hissed.

"You want to know the best opening line for a girl like Lianna?"

"Ad*aaamm*! Shhhhh!"

Adam has a big mouth. It was a major mistake to tell him I liked Lianna Walker. I mean, she's

14

fourteen. She wouldn't be caught dead with a seventh-grader like me.

"Hey, what's up?" Adam said, examining a salad.

I peered into his bowl. "Is something *in* there?"

"*No*! I mean, that's what you should say to *her*. 'Hey, what's up?' "

"That's it?"

"That's it."

"Adam, you're brilliant," I said, grabbing a roll and butter. "I mean, how do you *think* of these things? You have this *way* with words, you know?"

"Seriously, bro. I watch Lianna on the bus every day. I feel like I *know* her. She's the kind of girl who likes the straightforward type. Strong and silent."

"So I'll say nothing and flex my biceps."

Adam grabbed a plate full of orange glop off the hot lunch counter. "Hey, bananas wrapped in ham with cheese sauce again! Cool."

Adam is weird, but he can't help it. When he was a toddler he ate some wet cement on one of his dad's construction sites. His parents say he was never the same afterward. I do trust his opinions on some things, though. Like girls.

I mean, not that he's a big stud muffin or anything. He's not. And neither am I. And usually I don't really notice girls. Meaning, *notice* any more than anyone else. But, on the other hand, I don't *not* notice, if someone is worth noticing.

Am I making myself clear?

Anyway, Lianna was noticeable with a capital *N*. Shining, deep brown hair and huge eyes and a smile that could light up the schoolyard after dark. (Of course, I have never *been* in the school-yard after dark with Lianna, except in my dreams, but you know what I mean.)

"What's the other choice?" I asked Ms. Glupe, the lunch lady.

"Soy-liverwurst-and-olive spread on wheat bread with hummus on the side," she replied.

I took the bananas wrapped in ham with cheese sauce.

Since the fall, Hopnoodle Junior High had been using a low-cholesterol, high-protein "New Cuisine." Supposedly it was better for us than the mystery meats we used to have. But the real reason for it, according to my mom, was that it was cheaper.

School almost didn't happen that year in Hopnoodle. Money had run out, and the board almost closed us down. But too many people protested (*I* sure didn't), so we were open on an "emergency budget." A public meeting had been scheduled for that Tuesday night, so the grown-ups could all

16

argue about how to raise money. In the meantime, we all had to use old textbooks and go without paper towels in the boys' room.

And eat New Cuisine, which was so gross that everyone was losing weight.

Except Adam. He was five foot nine, one hundred sixty, and growing fast.

Adam leaned close to me as we left the lunch line and entered the cafeteria. "There she is," he mumbled. "Remember the line?"

I could see Lianna at a table across the room. She dug her fork into her orange lunch-glop, gagged, and looked about ready to hurl.

God, she was beautiful.

"You've got to be kidding," I said. "You *are* kidding?"

"She's *alone*," Adam observed.

"I know. And she's probably very happy that way."

"Follow me." Adam walked in front of me and sat directly opposite Lianna.

She looked at him for a split second. Suddenly she became interested in her lunch.

"Hey, Shawn!" Adam called over his shoulder. "Here's an empty seat. Right next to me and across from *Lianna Walker*!"

Thank you, Adam.

I sat where he said to. This time Lianna didn't

even look up. She was deeply involved in scraping the cheese sauce off the banana, which was not easy.

"Hi," Adam said nonchalantly.

Lianna didn't answer. This made Adam look like a fool, so *I* answered him. "Hi."

Adam nodded happily. "Hi."

Now Lianna looked up. "You guys really make interesting conversation."

I thought I could see a smile flickering across her face. My heart started beating heavily. I tried to remember Adam's advice. "Um . . . uh . . . er . . . hey, what's up?"

"Heyyyyy, dudes and dudette, mind if I join you?"

Without waiting for an answer, Buford dropped his tray next to Lianna's and sat down.

Lianna looked at him as if he had a toad growing out of his forehead. *"Dudette?"*

"I'm Buford Tutweiler," he said. "I'm doing Skool-2-Skool this week. What grade are you in?"

"None of your — " Lianna began.

"Ninth," Adam quickly cut in.

"Yeah? Me, too!" Buford lied.

I started to open my mouth, but Lianna spoke first. "Do you call girls *dudettes* at Pifflethorn?"

"Oh, I'm sorry, I guess I have a lot to learn, huh?" Buford opened a gold foil box of chocolates on his tray. "Truce. My mom gave me these, and I can't eat them all. Would you like some?"

Lianna looked at them warily. "Well, it's better than what I have for lunch."

"What kind do you like?" Buford asked. "I have mints and caramels, and — um . . ."

"I love caramels," Lianna said.

Buford confidently took one out and handed it to her. "Here. Sweets for the sweet."

Gag me.

"Can I have one?" Adam asked.

Buford shot him a look. "Do you *mind?*"

"Yuuuuck!" Lianna had taken a bite of the chocolate, and dark red stuff gooshed out onto her chin. "This is cherry cream!"

"Oops, let me clean it up," Buford said.

"I'll eat the rest!" Adam blurted out, grabbing it from her hand.

Buford bolted to his feet. "Hey, leave her alone!"

Adam stuffed the half-chocolate into his mouth. "Wassamatter?" he mumbled as he chewed. "You wannit back?"

He opened wide.

"Eeewww!" Lianna cried out.

"You pig!" Buford leaned across the table.

Adam laughed. "At least I don't lie about my grade."

"*Ooga trash!*"

Adam froze.

The tables next to us fell silent. Kids turned to look at Buford.

I should explain. To a Hopnoodlian, no insult is lower than "ooga trash." Especially when it comes from someone who lives in Pifflethorn.

Slowly Adam rose from his seat. I could practically see the smoke puffing from his ears. "What did you call me?" he said through gritted teeth.

"You heard me," Buford replied.

"*What did you call me?*"

"Ah-*OO*-gah! *OO*-gah!"

Big mistake, Buford.

Adam reached across the table and grabbed Buford's shirt. With his other hand he grabbed his lunch plate.

"Hey — let go — what are you — ?" Buford stammered.

Splat!

In one quick motion, Adam shoved the ham-and-cheese-sauce-covered banana right into Buford's face.

"You little — " Buford pick up a hunk of soy liverwurst and threw it at Adam.

"*Food fight!*" someone yelled.

A roll went flying over my head. A pat of butter

smacked Lianna in the left ear. I narrowly avoided a goopy, half-eaten banana.

"Stop!" Lianna yelled.

"Come on!" I said, grabbing her arm.

The two of us ran to the next table and hid underneath. A carton of apple juice hit the floor near us and splattered. Frank Mandolia went running into it and slid across the room, screaming. A peanut butter sandwich flew into Janice Taylor's milk, which fell off the table. Trevor Van Pelt had gathered cherry tomatoes and was pitching them one by one.

Mr. Nofziger, one of the teachers on duty, ran around shouting, "Children! Children!"

A hard-boiled egg beaned him from behind. His toupee went flying.

Finally the front door burst open and a voice boomed out: *"THE NEXT PERSON OUT OF A SEAT WILL BE SUSPENDED!"*

Yikes.

It was Ms. Stritch, our principal. The meanest, toughest person in the state. How tough? She'd had a brief acting career in Hollywood until she beat up Arnold Schwarzenegger over a parking space. So she went into education instead.

And we were lucky enough to have her.

Lianna and I scrambled onto a bench.

"WHO STARTED THIS?" Ms. Stritch demanded.

"*He* did!" Buford cried out, pointing to Adam.

"Did not!" Adam protested. "He called me — he called me — a bad name!" (No one in Hopnoodle ever likes to say the o. t. phrase.)

"I just . . . I just asked where the trash was," Buford whined, wiping the sauce off his face.

"That's a lie!" Adam called out.

But Ms. Stritch had Adam by the collar. "IN MY OFFICE AT ONCE, MR. FENSTER," she snarled. Then she shouted over her shoulder to the rest of us, *"I HAD BETTER SEE THIS PLACE SPOTLESS WHEN I RETURN WITH HIS CORPSE!"*

Great sense of humor, that Ms. Stritch.

She whisked Adam out the door. Around us, kids were scurrying with napkins and paper towels, wiping up whatever they could.

I smiled at Lianna. "Hey," I said nonchalantly. "What's up?"

She sneered. "You used that one already."

3

The Leap Year Lights

"Confetti," I said.

"Snow," Dad replied.

"Dandruff."

"Freckles."

"Zits."

Dad had parked the Weiner's Wieners van by the old field near my school. We were gazing through the sunroof, trying to find the best way to describe the stars.

Zits, I think, was our low point.

I took deep, deep breaths. For late February it was a pretty warm night, and the air was so clear and fresh you could almost drink it. Overhead the Milky Way arched across the sky like the stroke of a huge white paintbrush.

That was when I saw the flash of light. I sat up.

It streaked from right to left, growing more intense, changing in color from blue to red to blinding white.

Then it disappeared over the crest of evergreen trees at the western edge of town.

"Whoa, did you see that?" I asked.

Dad let out a long, low whistle. "The Leap Year Lights," he said under his breath.

"Huh?"

"It's an old legend. Every four years, on February twenty-ninth, angels descend to Earth in a burst of light to visit one place that needs help the most."

My heart started to quicken. "Really?"

Dad smiled and started up the engine. "Nahhh, I just made it up. Gotcha, huh?"

I slumped back in my seat. "Ha-ha."

As we drove away, I secretly kept my eyes on the area behind the trees.

The light was dimming slowly.

4

Buford's Business Deal

"Uh, *hello*? Where am I supposed to wipe my hands around here?"

Only Buford could make a simple question like that sound obnoxious.

Adam and I had been minding our own business in the boys' room. It was Tuesday, so Adam had had a whole day to recover from Ms. Stritch. He had been lucky. She hadn't tortured him or made him write an essay on manners or shouted in his face with her tuna-salad breath.

All she did was threaten him with suspension if he made any more trouble with "that Toot-wheeler boy."

I cracked up when I heard how she pronounced Buford's name. Boy, was I dying to call him that. But I kept it inside all day.

Now, in the bathroom, Buford was standing over the sink with his hands dripping. (I guess no one in Pifflethorn had told him about the paper towel crisis at HJHS.) He had this scrunched-up, disgusted expression, as if he'd been forced to spend the day in the sewer system.

Which, if you knew the Hopnoodle bathrooms, wasn't too far from the truth.

"Earth to nerds, Earth to nerds," Buford said. "Where do I wipe my hands? Come in, please."

I could tell Adam was trying really hard not to flatten him.

"Blow on them," Adam mumbled.

"Uh, say it again, louder and funnier?"

"Let's go," I said, grabbing Adam's arm.

To my surprise, he came with me.

"Guess I could use your hair," Buford called after us.

Adam spun around. "Your own is too greasy, huh, pizza face?"

Buford flung his hands at us, sending a light spray into our faces. "April showers."

I thought Adam was going to haul off and slug him. Instead he calmly went back to the sink, turned on the water full blast, and stuck his finger in the spigot.

A gusher shot out at Buford. He jumped away, but he was hit square in the pants.

"Oops," said Adam.

For a long moment, Buford stared at the stain below his belt. When he looked up, his face was red.

I tried not to laugh. Really I did. But I couldn't help it.

"Oh, you think this is *funny*?" Buford bellowed, pointing a wet finger in my face.

Adam pushed Buford's hand away and stood eye to eye with him. "Yes, *Tootwheeler*. We do. HA. HA. HEE. HEE."

"Uh, Adam?" I said. "It's almost time for math. Maybe we should go."

"I wonder if Ms. Stritch will find this funny, too, when I tell her who did it," Buford said.

Adam gulped.

"She's just waiting for you to slip up, Adam. She's probably already got your name on a suspension slip."

"Who told you — ?"

"This won't look good on your *permanent record*."

Ugh. I hate those words. I could see Adam's life flashing before his eyes. He was turning three shades of pale. "You wouldn't do that," he said.

"Not in these pants." Buford began unbuckling his belt. "Give me yours."

"Whaaaaat?" Adam replied.

"You heard me."

"Uh-uh," Adam said. "No way."

"Oh, Ms. *Striii-itch!*" Buford sang out.

"Okay, okay. I'll do it!"

Grumbling, Adam quickly changed pants with Buford.

The problem was, Buford was about two sizes smaller. His pant legs soared high above Adam's socks, and Adam couldn't close up the waistband. (I hate to say it, but *his* pants kind of looked cool on Buford, all baggy and bunched up.)

Buford howled with laughter. *"Lookin' good, dude!"*

"I have to go to *class* like this?" Adam moaned.

"Look, Buford," I said. "You punished Adam enough. You don't have to go to Ms. Stritch now."

Buford pretended he was deep in thought, which made him look even stupider. "Well . . . my feelings were awfully hurt," he replied. "And you still haven't answered my question — "

"About the paper towels?" Adam asked. "There are none in the whole school! *I* can't help that!"

"Why not?" Buford said. "You have *stores* in Hopnoodle, don't you?"

"Fine, I'll buy some," Adam said. "And I'll give you a jumbo pack, okay? Are we even now?"

"I have a better idea. We can all go into business. You, me, and . . . *E.T.* over here."

28

That was me he meant. And I didn't appreciate it.

"*You* buy them," Buford went on. "*You* stand by the sink and hold them. Shawn can rip off the sheets, one per customer."

"What do *you* do?" I asked.

Buford grinned goonily. "*I*, being the brains of the outfit, collect the money. Five cents a sheet sound good?"

"Cram it, Buford!" I said.

"Your choice." Buford headed for the door. "How sad for Adam, though. About his *permanent record*."

"Wait!" Adam shot back. "If I do this, will you promise to stay away from Stritch?"

A slow grin spread across Buford's face. "We start tomorrow," he said. "And get the really good, thick kind."

5

The End of Our School as We Know It

"**A**nd whereas, on this day, the village of Hop-noodle does heretoforth bite the rutabaga, we blubber-blabber our peas and carrots sideways into the swampgrass . . ."

Okay, those were not the *exact* words of Mayor Glipnik at the village meeting that night. But it was close enough. I had a hard time paying attention.

Usually I don't go to these things. But Dad had volunteered at the last minute to help on the refreshment committee, and he made me go with him.

I was not happy. Especially since my little brother, the Newt, didn't have to go. (His real name is Nathaniel, and he's eight, but he had bug eyes like a newt when he was born, so I call him that, even though he hates it.)

I called Adam right away. His parents were going, and he agreed to come along, too. So it wasn't a total waste.

The village hall was packed. The mayor had written the words *School Budget Crisis* in huge letters on a blackboard.

As he rambled on, Dad and Adam and I worked like crazy. "Thank you, and enjoy your wiener!" Adam kept saying over and over.

". . . so before we discuss the school budget *per se*," Mayor Glipnik droned on, "I have been advised of an important development concerning said topic. Here to tell us about it is none other than Mr. Horst N. Petard!"

Oh, groan. Another windbag.

Horst N. Petard is the biggest man in Pifflethorn. Width-wise, that is. He must weigh about three hundred fifty pounds. Cash-wise, too. He owns half the town. And some of Hopnoodle.

Our hot dog customers straggled to their seats. A hush went through the crowd. I gulped down a soda.

The stage creaked as Mr. Petard waddled to the mike. "Ladies and gentlemen," he snuffled. "When I moved to Pifflethorn, I had only five dollars and a melted Chunky in my pocket. Over the years, my pot grew a millionfold."

"That's for sure," Adam whispered.

I nearly spit out my soda laughing.

"I'm here tonight to make you an offer," Mr. Petard continued. "An offer to do for Hopnoodle what I've done for Pifflethorn. I have been contacted by Ghiek Industries, a new, exciting, family-run company — and they are willing to buy the Hopnoodle Ooga Horn factory to use for their business, effective immediately."

Gasps erupted all over the room.

Adam was cracking up. "*Geek* Industries?"

"Order!" Mayor Glipnik shouted.

"Ghiek is a good, sound company," Mr. Petard droned on. "One that will put Hopnoodle on the map. Provide jobs. Security. Prosperity. Solidity. Liquidity — "

What kind of company is it?" my dad called out.

"Only the biggest growth field in the country!" Mr. Petard replied. "Biotechnology. Genetic engineering."

A few people let out groans.

"Just what we need!" shouted one man. "Mutant diseases flying around."

"Monsters!" screamed someone else.

"Little yucky germs!" squeaked another voice.

"Let him speak!" Dad yelled.

32

"Think of it," Mr. Petard said. "Hopnoodle on the rise! Tourism. New construction. You'll all be able to hold your heads up high again. *I am talking big money, my friends!*"

"And boy, do we need it!" shouted Mr. Fenster from the crowd. (He's a construction contractor, but he's had to work part-time for an earthworm farm ever since Hopnoodle started going down the tubes.)

"Now maybe they'll fix up the school," I whispered to Adam.

"Or build a new one," he replied.

One woman stood up and said, "But the factory is so close to the junior high! What if the little mutant bugs crawl out and invade our children?"

Mr. Petard chuckled. "I assure you, Ghiek Industries will be using state-of-the-art germ containment. In fact, I am so certain of that, I have drawn up plans for a condominium complex to be built on that site next to the factory, ma'am. Hopnoodle will need housing for the great influx of new workers, and this would be *prime* land."

"Hold it!" Dad called out. "What about the school?"

Mr. Petard scowled. "I took a tour of that school, and frankly, I was appalled! It's outdated and dangerous. I counted at least fifteen fire-hazard violations in the front hallway alone! I ask you, do you want your children to be taught in these conditions?"

"No!" a chorus rang out.

"Good! Because in the *new* Hopnoodle Village, children will never again spend a day in a building that has no paper towels!"

The crowd cheered.

"Yeah!" Adam said. We were both nudging each other in the ribs. This was sounding great.

"I have contacted the state authorities, who will be visiting soon to discuss condemnation," Mr. Petard announced. "I say, the sooner we raze it to the ground, the better!"

"Yeeee-hahhhh!" Adam whooped.

"Whoa, not so fast!" Dad said. "Don't you *own* the land under the school, Mr. Petard?"

"Well, er, yes, in fact, I do," Mr. Petard harrumphed.

"And I guess if you tear down the school and build condos there, you'll make much more money," Dad continued.

"Indeed, sir, I'm a businessman! But let me remind you, this is for the good of Hopnoodle. And your children will benefit enormously."

"I'm all for that," Dad shot back. "But where will they go to school?"

"I have made arrangements with some of my

land interests in the next town. An extension to their middle school will be ready by September." Mr. Petard smiled triumphantly. "There will be ample room to transfer all Hopnoodle Junior High students to Pifflethorn."

My jaw hit the floor.

6

The Geeks

*C*link.
    Rrrrrip!
"Thank you for your business."
Clink.
Rrrrrip!
"Thank you for your business."
Boy, did I feel ridiculous.

As each nickel clinked into Buford's cup, I ripped off a sheet of paper towel. Adam, who was standing at attention with two fingers in each side of the roll, had to do the thanking. He was so furious, he practically spat his words out.

We were in the boys' room near the front hallway. Buford had made us show up before the first bell, ready for the early birds.

Adam and I were still smarting from the news of the night before. A transfer to Pifflethorn? My week there had been the worst of my life. I couldn't wait to get away from those snotty, spoiled kids. The idea of going there *every day* was horrifying. I could barely sleep that night. I had dreams of the Pifflethorn kids leading us all around in dog collars.

Clink.

Rrrrrip!

"Thank you for your business."

Which wasn't too far from what was happening right then.

In the hallway, voices grew louder and angrier as kids arrived at school. Some of the kids who came into the bathroom were ballistic. *Nobody* had anything nice to say about Pifflethorn.

But Buford didn't care. As long as they paid their nickels.

Most of our classmates were grateful for the paper towels. Except Frank Mandolia, who thought the service was worth three cents, called us a rip-off, and cracked up at his own joke. Trevor Van Pelt asked if he was supposed to leave a tip. (Buford, of course, said yes.) Fred Bilecki argued about the money, then wiped his hands on my pants.

And that was just in the fifteen minutes before homeroom.

Buford was already dreaming up grand schemes for the future. "If you guys play your cards right," he said, "you can have a piece of the business. See, you each take a bathroom of your own and hire a staff. Then you give me the money and I pay you, oh, ten percent."

"*Ten* percent?" Adam protested.

"You're right, that's a lot. Maybe five. Then we get Lianna involved in a girls' division, which splits the profits with me fifty-fifty — "

Suddenly the loud voices in the hallway fell silent. Then a burst of laughter floated into the bathroom.

The boys' room emptied.

"Stay here," Buford said, pocketing the nickels. "I'll be right back."

Adam waited until he left, then stuffed the roll of paper towels under his arm. "Let's go!"

Together we raced into the hallway. A throng of kids had gathered around the front door in a semicircle. They were mumbling and giggling and chattering away. Some of them looked embarrassed.

"Uh-oh," Adam muttered. "Did Waldo Wigglesworth drop a dog turd on the floor again?"

I sniffed. "Nahh."

We elbowed our way through the crowd, being

careful not to let Buford see us. Fortunately that wasn't too hard, because the place was packed.

When we reached the middle, we stopped.

And stared.

It was not a dog turd.

Or a fight.

Or anything else I'd ever seen before.

Three kids stood there. Two boys and a girl. Looking around. Smiling.

But what kids.

They had greenish-brown hair and Coke-bottle glasses. Each was grinning widely, showing teeth covered with braces that looked like the grill of a car. They had no coats, and they wore shorts that showed their toothpick-thin legs.

And boy, were they ever pale. Their skin was almost bluish.

In one hand, each of them carried a book bag. In the other hand, each held a different, strange-looking fruit.

No one was saying a word to them. The more they looked nervously around, flashing their heavy-metal smiles, the more kids giggled.

"Yo, *what* are *you*?"

Leave it to Buford. He pushed through the throng and marched up to the kids.

The tallest one said, "I am Sylvester."

"I'm Chester," chimed in the shortest one.

"Esther," added the girl.

"We're new here," Sylvester said. "Our father is Lester Ghiek, who owns Ghiek Industries. We are the Ghieks."

That did it.

"*GEEEEEEKS!*" someone shouted.

Frank made a scrunched-up face and began marching around like a chicken. A couple of other kids kept repeating, "Duh . . . duh" while walking into each other. Trevor messed up his hair and stood next to Sylvester, grinning.

Nice welcome.

Buford grabbed a wrinkled little fruit out of Chester's hand. "What's this thing?"

"A fig," Chester explained with a smile. "According to American custom, we are bringing fruits to our teacher."

"I have a kumquat," Esther added.

"An Ugli fruit," Sylvester said.

"Foreigners!" Buford bellowed. He grabbed all three fruits and started juggling them. One by one, they fell to the floor.

"Oh, sorry," Buford said as the Ghieks kneeled to pick them up. "Gee, I guess you need paper towels. But don't worry. They're only five cents each. YO, ADAM AND SHAWN! CUSTOMERS!"

"This is cruel," I said to Adam.

Adam stepped forward. "Leave them alone," he said.

Buford laughed. "Oh, you're their hero, huh? Guess that makes sense. Their dad is the reason you turkeys get to go to my school next year."

"*Whaaaat?*" Trevor exclaimed.

"Read my lips, birdbrains," Buford said. "Ghiek Industries. Recognize the name? That's the company. Say hello to your future, boys and girls."

The Ghieks were beaming, as if Buford had just given them a huge compliment.

"Get 'em!" Fred Bilecki yelled.

"Go back to Geekland!" screamed Janice Taylor.

Everyone started talking and shouting at once.

"ALL RIGHT, BREAK IT UP!" Ms. Stritch's voice swallowed up the noise. "WHAT'S GOING ON? WALDO, IF YOU — "

She burst through the throng. But when she took one look at the three strangers, she broke into a big smile. "YOU MUST BE LESTER'S CHILDREN. COME RIGHT IN TO MY OFFICE. I HAVE A FEW WELCOMING PRESENTS FOR YOU."

Sylvester, Chester, and Esther Ghiek ambled through the crowd behind Ms. Stritch, smiling and nodding as if nothing had happened. They were holding their squashed fruits, which dribbled a trail on the tiled floor.

Buford spotted us. He quickly ripped three paper towels off and gave one to each Ghiek.

"Thank you," they said politely as they walked toward the office.

Buford stood there, fuming. *"Hey! Where's my fifteen cents?"*

7

That Smell, That Glow . . .

"**A**S MOST OF YOU KNOW, TOMORROW I WILL BE LEAVING FOR A WEEK-LONG EDUCATIONAL SYMPOSIUM IN MIL-WAUKEE! MR. DABNEY WILL BE TAKING MY PLACE! I EXPECT YOU WILL TREAT OUR NEW STUDENTS, THE GHIEKS, WITH OUR TRADITIONAL HOPNOODLE HOSPI-TALITY!"

Ms. Stritch's voice boomed through the school auditorium later that day. She wasn't using a mike, but she was still too loud.

Normally, we would be dancing for joy at her news. But she hadn't called the assembly just to tell us about her trip. She had officially announced our banishment to Pifflethorn next year — *if* the state officials agreed.

In the seat next to me, Adam was in nuclear meltdown. "No way. I'll move. I'll run away from home. I'll jump a ship to Iceland. I'll send a letter bomb to the Pifflethorn principal."

"They *do* have good courses," I whispered.

"I hate Jerry Lewis movies," he grumbled.

"We'll have paper towels," I said.

"Wow, that sure will be worth those two bus trips a day."

"Adam, you already take a bus."

"MR. FERGUSON! DO YOU HAVE SOMETHING YOU WANT TO SHARE WITH THE REST OF US?"

Gulp.

I shook my head and sat up straight in my seat.

(I don't know about you, but I hate when teachers ask that question. I mean, if you had something to share, why would you be whispering?)

From two rows up, Lianna Walker looked over her shoulder at me as if I were a convicted serial killer. That was when I noticed the person in the seat next to her was Sylvester Ghiek.

As she turned back around, she brushed his shoulder. I could see her lips mouthing, "Sorry."

Adam dug a pen and a candy wrapper out of his pockets and scribbled a note to me:

Did you see the smile she gave him?

I nodded.

More furious scribbling.

EL GEEKO IS MOVING IN ON YOUR GIRL,
BRO! I say we keep an eye on him!!!!!!

I nodded again and gave him back the note.

Adam seemed more and more concerned about Lianna every day.

Boy, was I lucky to have him looking out for my best interests.

I first noticed the funny smell the next day, in math.

It was a burning, electrical kind of a smell. It reminded me of the time the blender motor blew in our house. I didn't think much of it, though. I figured the custodian's vacuum cleaner had blown up or something.

But as the class dragged on, it just got stronger.

"Do you smell that?" I finally whispered to Adam, who was sitting in front of me.

"Yeah," Adam whispered back. "I figured you were burning brain cells."

"Ha-ha."

It definitely wasn't me. It was coming from the right-hand side, where Chester Ghiek was sitting. (He and Esther were twins, and I seemed to have one or the other in every class.) Chester was writing furiously in his notebook.

". . . so who can give me the answer to question number seven? Hmmm?" said Mr. Zoster, my math teacher. "Chester?"

"Oh!" Chester looked up. "Uh, pardon me? Number what?"

Adam leaned back and said into my ear, *"Hey, he's normal!"*

"Am I going too slow for you, Chester?" Mr. Zoster asked kindly, as he picked up Chester's paper. "What are you writing?"

"I was merely calculating various probabilities of particle diffusion based on the Schrödinger wave equation," Chester replied.

Mr. Zoster turned ghostly white and put the paper back down. "I . . . see. Um, Chester, would you stay to see me after class?" He began sniffing loudly. "And, uh, will someone open a window while I get the custodian?"

I looked at Adam. He looked at me.

Now the smell was overpowering.

After class, Adam and I stopped outside the door.

"It's Chester," I said.

"What's Chester?" Adam asked.

"The smell. It's him. I know it."

46

Adam rolled his eyes. "I smelled like that once when my underwear elastic melted in the dryer. Don't worry about it."

"Adam, the Ghieks are not normal — "

"Look, I don't want to be late for gym. You want to sleep over tonight?"

"Why?"

"I figured out the problem with Lianna. She's *tired* by lunch period. Believe me, in the morning she's much nicer. If you sleep over, you take my bus with me tomorrow, and we'll sit behind her — "

"No, Adam. No. Don't embarrass me, okay?"

"Okay, okay, I won't." He shrugged. "We can play my new Sega Genesis game."

"Deal. I'll ask my mom and dad."

Adam ran off to gym. I had to go the opposite way, to social studies.

I ran and ran, weaving through the crowded hallway. And suddenly, I was running in darkness.

Just like that, the lights were out. I skidded to a stop in front of the computer lab. Orange auxiliary lights popped on at the ends of the hallways.

Kids started screaming, "Blackout!" at the top of their lungs.

"BOOOOOO-AH-HA-HA-HA!" shouted a deep voice.

"Buford, stop it!" That was Lianna.

Whomp! I saw Buford's flapping arms only a split second before he knocked me to the ground.

"BOOOOOO-AH-HA-HA-HA!" He jumped away, bounding into people left and right.

I stood up. All around me, kids were going crazy. The hallway was a mass of crisscrossing shadows.

Keeping one hand on the tiled wall, I groped my way to the nearest door, the computer lab.

I pushed it open and stepped inside. It was quiet and dark and empty. Whew. I felt around and found a chair.

But the moment I plopped into it, I knew I wasn't alone.

Esther Ghiek was in the far corner, fiddling around with the guts of one of the computers.

I could see her pretty clearly.

She was glowing.

8

Buford Meets His Match

Blink.

The overhead fluorescents flickered on again.

Esther looked up. She nodded when she saw me. "Hello, I am Esther — "

"Is everyone all right?" Mr. Dabney ran into the room, huffing and puffing. Behind him was Mr. Trumple, the custodian.

"I'd stay away from that computer," Mr. Trumple warned Esther. "We had some huge power drop in this room. Knocked out all the circuit breakers."

"Yes," Esther said, quickly putting the computer back together. "I did not expect its amperage to be so low."

"You *what*?" Mr. Trumple said.

"It will not happen again."

Esther stood up and walked out of the room. She looked pretty weird, on those skinny little legs, kind of lunging from side to side.

Mr. Dabney and Mr. Trumple went over to the computer. Mr. Trumple poked and prodded the wires, tapped the keyboard, and stared for a long time at the monitor. "You know anything about computers?" he asked Mr. Dabney.

"Nahh."

"Me neither."

As they walked out, Mr. Dabney said, "Get to class, Shawn."

Right. Sure.

Class.

I was too freaked out to move. Something was very, very wrong here.

Adam and I jogged down the hallway during lunch period. "*How* was she glowing?" Adam asked. "Like one of those human body things at the museum? Could you, like, see her pancreas and stuff?"

"She was wearing *clothes*, Adam," I said. "Anyway, it was kind of a *soft* glow. You know, like those fluorescent stickers you hold up to the light?"

We burst through the boys' room door. Buford

was tapping his feet and staring at his watch. "Where *were* you? I had to hold the towels myself for two people."

"Poor baby," Adam said.

"You're supposed to have five minutes for your lunch. *Five.* Not seven minutes and twenty-three seconds."

"They had pork chops," Adam explained. "And they forgot to give us chainsaws to cut them. Okay?"

Buford shoved the paper towels at him.

The boys' room door opened. We took our positions.

"Why are we doing this anyway?" I said under my breath. "Ms. Stritch isn't here."

"*Because*, smart guy," Buford replied, "she gave expletive instructions to Mr. Dabney to boot Adam out if he bothered me again."

"Ex*plicit*," I said. "Not *expletive*."

"Watch your language."

"English, what's yours?"

"Ssshhh!" said Adam.

From the toilet stall, we could hear gentle splashing noises. "Did you see who went in there?" Adam whispered.

"No," Buford and I answered.

The stall door opened.

Sylvester Ghiek walked out, carrying a soda can.

"What did you do, take a bath?" Buford asked.

Sylvester held up the can. "No. I merely collected some hydrogen dioxide in this receptacle."

"Collected *whaaa* in *whaaa*?" Buford said.

"Water," I informed him. "In that can."

"Get outta here," Buford said skeptically.

"Yes. That was my plan." Sylvester turned toward the door.

"Hey, not so fast." Buford ran and put a hand on his shoulder. "You just stuck your hand in the toilet. Don't you need a paper towel?"

"No, thank you," Sylvester said. "The supply had a coliform count below that which is considered unsanitary."

"The water was clean," I translated for Buford.

Buford took a menacing step forward. "You think you're smart, huh? You think you can duck into the john and sneak out without paying for a paper towel?"

"But I did not — "

Buford stepped over to Adam, ripped off a sheet, and handed it to Sylvester. "That'll be a quarter. Five for you, fifteen for the sheets you and your geeky brother and sister skipped out on, and a nickel interest. And don't tell me you can't afford it."

"I wish to exercise my right of refusal, guaranteed by the democratic philosophy of government."

Buford looked at me.

"He says, no, it's a free country," I explained.

Well, Buford nearly exploded. He shoved Sylvester against the wall and stuffed the paper towel in his shirt pocket. "Here, you ugly little sewer rat. If I don't see twenty-five cents by — "

What happened next was so fast I can't really describe it. All I know was that Buford ended up pinned to the floor faceup, with Sylvester sitting on his chest.

"Wha — hey — get off — " Buford gasped.

"You have been showing signs of hostility," Sylvester said.

"Giiig — glub — aaaa — " Buford replied.

"My brother and sister have perceived these signs, as well. Perhaps we are, by our mere presence, unwittingly taking something of value from others, for which we may be able to provide restitution."

"Oof — what — gack — "

"Get off him!" I shouted, pulling Sylvester away.

Sylvester calmly stood up.

Buford was breathing heavily. His face was bright red. "What'd he say?"

"I don't know," I replied.

"May I fulfill some need for you, so that you and your schoolmates will be our friends?" Sylvester asked.

"What are you, a genie?" Adam asked.

"No. A Sylvester. S-Y-L — "

Buford sat up. "Listen, the second-floor boys' room needs paper towels — "

"Stuff it, Buford," Adam said. "Yo, Sylvester, can you turn him into a cockroach?"

"I know!" I said. "You can renovate the school, so it doesn't have to be torn down. I mean, if your dad's company gets, like, super successful, couldn't they spare a little money?"

Sylvester shook his head. "Sadly, no. Mr. Petard intends to build on this land, and he owns it. From my study of American real estate conflicts, I sense the lack of the one ingredient that is necessary to persuade landowners to act against their own interests."

"I'm lost," Buford said.

"What's the ingredient?" Adam asked.

"Humiliation," Sylvester replied. "Large-scale protest that attracts media coverage."

Adam groaned. "Great. How are we going to do that?"

Sylvester grinned. "Leave it to me."

9

You Are What You Eat

"**H**um-de-dum-de-dum-dum. Why don't we sit here, Shawn?"

It was early Friday morning. Fresh from our sleepover, Adam and I had boarded the school bus. Adam was cheerfully pointing to the seat behind Lianna.

"*Don't . . . do . . . this,*" I growled.

"Yep. Sure is a beautiful day, Shawn."

As soon as we slid into the seats, Lianna turned around. "Those are saved."

"Oh, hi!" Adam said, with this strange goggle-eyed expression that I guess was supposed to look like surprise.

"Hi," I added weakly.

"Those seats are saved," she repeated.

"Oh, uh, sure, uh, we'll just . . . move," Adam

replied, poking me in the ribs. *"Say something,"* he whispered.

" 'Bye," I said.

Adam groaned and shook his head.

We moved into the seat behind and stared glumly out the window.

The bus trundled on to the next stop. In walked Sylvester, Esther, and Chester Ghiek. Each of them held a bulging shopping bag.

"I thought they just . . . *levitated* to school," I muttered.

"Hi!" Lianna waved enthusiastically to Sylvester, patting the spot next to her on the seat.

"Pleasant weather conditions," Sylvester said.

Chester and Esther nodded a greeting to us and plopped into the seat between us and Lianna.

Sylvester spotted us, too. "Hello. I believe we have devised a strategy for the conflict we discussed in the bathroom."

"Terrific," Adam said.

Lianna pulled Sylvester down into the seat next to her. "Did you do the English homework? I could not get through that play!"

"Julius Caesar is a cautionary tale of betrayal and corruption," Sylvester replied.

"That's good . . . I like that," Lianna said, scribbling in her notebook. "I got to the part where the guy says, 'Beware the ides of March.'

What are ides? Is that, like, old English for *ideas*, or *idiots* or something?"

"The ides is simply the fifteenth of the month," Sylvester explained.

"Can you believe this?" Adam whispered. "He does her homework for her!"

"Adam, chill, okay?" I said. "It's none of our business."

We sat there silently. Behind us, some kids started throwing spitballs around and laughing like crazy. Adam is a spitball expert, but he didn't seem to care.

I reached into my backpack for something to read, when Adam started sniffing.

"What's that?" he asked.

I caught a faint whiff of that strange burning smell, mixed with the scent of baked bread and chocolate.

Adam peered over Esther and Chester's seat. His eyes lit up.

"Whoa, what a stash of food," he whispered.

"*Adammmm* . . ."

Esther and Chester were busily tapping the keys of their calculators. Slowly, Adam reached between them, over the seat.

I sat up straight and watched. His hand went silently into a paper bag with handles.

When it came back out, it was holding a huge

bar of butter crunch. "Yum, I *love* this stuff!" he said.

"Hey, you can't just — "

Yes, he could. The butter crunch disappeared into his smiling mouth. "Ish oh-hey. Ey ha rosh mo."

"Huh?"

He swallowed. "It's okay. They have lots more. Candy, fruits, nuts, bread, muffins, cake, granola. It's incredible. Want some?"

"No! Adam, will you keep your hands to yourself?"

"Huuuh?" Adam turned to me slowly. His face looked kind of washed out and blank, as if he were about to puke.

Slowly he lifted his hands face-high, then clasped them to his chest.

"Uh, Adam? What are you doing?"

"Keeping my hands to myself," he said.

"Cut it out."

Adam reached into his pocket and took out a Swiss army knife.

"Whoa, put it away!" I said. "That's not funny."

Adam quickly put his knife back and stared straight ahead.

"Adam, are you okay?"

"Sure."

I peered over the seat into Esther's food bag. "Wow. What was in that candy bar?"

That got Esther's attention. She looked into her bag, then back at us. Her green hair spikes seemed to stiffen. "One is missing. Did he eat it?"

"Yes, and he's sorry," I said.

Esther made a face. I think she was smiling. "He will recover in approximately twenty-four hours." She looked at Adam. "Do not touch another item in my bag, or in those of my brothers, ever again."

"Yes," Adam said dreamily.

"And be careful what you ask him to do," Esther said to me.

"What happened to him?" I asked. "Is he under some kind of mind control?"

"The food was not meant for him," was all Esther said before she turned back to her calculator.

Adam was just sitting there. Smiling stupidly, still holding his hands to his chest.

"Adam," I said, "would you please put your hands down?"

Adam's hands dropped into his lap.

"Uh . . . Adam?" I took a deep breath. "Will you please bounce in your seat?"

Adam bounced.

"Stop."

He stopped.

"Make a burping noise."

"*Rrrrrrroup!*"

"Knock it off!" yelled Mr. Bandolucci, the bus driver.

Adam began pelting his face with his math book.

"Stop!" I said.

Adam put the book down. He still had this dumb smile. He let out a sudden giggle.

Now, I *know* Adam. I know what he's capable of. I did not trust this strange behavior. For all I knew, he had gotten together with the Ghieks and planned all this, just to rank on me.

"Adam," I said firmly. "Kiss the bus driver."

Adam stood up. He shuffled his way around my knees and went into the aisle.

Mr. Bandolucci looked into his rearview mirror. "Hey, where do you think you're going?" he barked.

Adam walked right up to him, knelt, and planted a big kiss on his beard-stubbly cheek.

10

Geek Food

*S*creeeeeek!

The bus careened left and right.

Outside cars were honking like crazy.

Inside the kids were losing it — falling into the aisle, shrieking with laughter.

Mr. Bandolucci's face was bright red. He struggled to find a grip on the steering wheel. "What the — *sit down*! You trying to cause an accident?"

Adam obediently returned to his seat, to a chorus of hooting and cheering and kissing noises.

With a screech of brakes, Mr. Bandolucci stopped the bus at the curb. He rose from his seat and began walking down the aisle.

Boy, was he steaming. "Okay, who put him up to this?"

Silence.

"This was some kind of dare, right? I know you -kids. Who did it?" His eyes fixed on me. "Was it *you*?"

I swallowed hard.

"Please do not blame him," Esther spoke up. "Adam ate one of these and temporarily lost his willpower."

She held out the bag toward Mr. Bandolucci.

He reached inside. Cautiously he pulled out a small blueberry muffin and examined it. "You think you're funny or something?"

"It's yours," Esther said. "With our compliments. As an . . . apology."

Scowling, Mr. Bandolucci popped the muffin in his mouth. "Well, thanks," he said, spitting muffin crumbs as he spoke, "but I want to make one thing clear. I don't allow troublemakers on my bus! So — "

Just like that, he stopped. His eyes became glassy. I thought he was going to pass out.

"Mr. Bandolucci," Chester said gently. "Return to your driving."

Mr. Bandolucci gave a funny little high-pitched laugh, spun on his heels, walked back to his seat, and started up the bus.

I looked around. I have never seen so many gaping mouths in my life.

Esther tucked the bag in the seat next to her.

"Thank you," I said.

"This was not supposed to be common knowledge," she whispered, turning back to her calculator.

Genetic engineering, I said to myself as I stepped off the bus with Adam. That's what happened. Ghiek Industries had put mutant mind-control DNA — or whatever — into the candy.

But why?

"Adam," I said. "Listen to me. Call home. Tell your mom you feel sick. Ask her to pick you up. When you get there, stay in your room until tomorrow morning. Do you understand?"

"No problem!" Laughing crazily, Adam skipped toward the front door, heading for the pay phones inside.

On the way, he passed the three Ghieks. They were alone, talking to one another by the front door. Lianna had wandered away from Sylvester to meet up with some friends.

I ran up to the Ghieks. "Okay, guys. I don't know who you are or how you managed to do this, but you better start giving me some answers."

"I am merely carrying out the wish you expressed in the boys' — " Sylvester began.

"How? By feeding everybody mutant junk food and brainwashing them?"

"Not everyone," Esther replied softly. "Merely teachers and administrators."

"Are you crazy? Give this stuff to *Mr. Petard*, not the teachers. They're on our side! They *want* the school to stay open. See, they have these things called *jobs* — "

"No, Shawn," Chester interrupted. "Mr. Petard has secretly arranged job offers for them in the new Pifflethorn school, at a higher wage. He confided this to our father, Lester Ghiek."

"The staff *prefers* the school to be torn down," Sylvester added.

"Yo! What's in the *baaa-ag*, dudes?"

I spun around. With his usual perfect timing, Buford was bounding toward us, out of a crowd of kids near the front door.

"Is that the magic food? The stuff that makes you obey every command?"

Esther backed away. "This is not to be handled by students."

"Heyyy, chill, Esther. I can help you make a *fortune* on this stuff."

"*Taste* some first, Buford," I quickly suggested.

Esther gave me a harsh look. "Shawn, we must control the use of these — "

With a sudden lunge, Buford grabbed her bag.

Out of nowhere, two other goons grabbed Sylvester's and Chester's bags.

"Hey! Look what we have!" Buford shouted, running toward the front door.

The three Ghieks and I tore off after them.

But Buford and his sidekicks disappeared into the crowd. The next moment, candy bars and bags of granola were flying into the air.

"Remember, everybody," Buford shouted, *"don't eat any of it yourselves!"*

"Stop!" I shouted.

The kids ran into the school, screaming, laughing, and playing catch with the food.

They left the bags outside.

Empty.

11

Feeding the Teachers

We raced after them.

"What are they going to do with the food?" Esther shouted.

Her hair was turning orange. Somehow I knew this meant she was afraid.

"How should I know?" I replied.

We passed by the principal's office. Mr. Dabney was munching on a cupcake. Mrs. Romney, the secretary, was eating a donut.

"Don't!" I shouted.

They both stopped in mid-bite.

"Too late!" Chester said.

We ran to the first classroom, room 103. Mr. Asquith was happily tossing jellybeans into his mouth. "Want some?" he asked his students.

"*No!*" they all shouted.

"Suit yourself," he said, shoving in another fistful.

They knew. All the kids knew. They were feeding the teachers on purpose. Sabotaging the school.

Ruining everything.

I turned to the Ghieks. "Break up! You go left, you go right, you go upstairs!"

Mr. Asquith began running in crazy patterns.

"Not you!" I shouted to him.

He stopped. The class was howling. *Screeching.*

"Hey, chill!" I yelled.

Mr. Asquith began shivering.

"Auuuugghh!" My heart was sinking. This was wrong. All wrong.

I had to find the teachers who hadn't eaten. Warn them. Get them to contain the damage.

I kept running.

Room 105. Ms. Whitney and her assistant teacher were splitting an apple crumb cake.

Room 107. Ms. Petersell and her students were playing catch with a blackboard eraser. She had a lollipop hanging out of her mouth.

Science lab. Mr. Nofziger was dancing with a life-size plastic skeleton. An empty granola bag was on his desk.

Computer lab. Nintendo on every screen.

A rap song blared out of the administration office. Inside, four guidance counselors were singing along, using their telephone receivers as mikes.

Then I heard voices coming from the gym:

"Lay up!"

"Hit the boards!"

"Dribble!"

"Three pointer!"

"Atta boy!"

Normal sounds. *Normal sounds!*

I sprinted inside.

The students were in their street clothes, sitting in the bleachers.

Mr. Armstrong, our gym teacher, was alone on the court. Following all the instructions that were yelled to him.

"Yo, bounce it off your head!" someone shouted.

I didn't want to watch anymore.

I collapsed onto the floor. All around me, the school sounded like a total loony bin.

Sylvester clattered down the stairs at the end of the hallway. "It's taking effect!" he shouted.

"No kidding!" I replied.

He sat down next to me. "We must think."

Chester and Esther came running down the hall toward us. All three of the Ghieks seemed tired. Their hair looked as if it were turning gray.

"Any survivors?" I asked.

"If by that you mean teachers who have not succumbed to the food," Esther said, "no."

"Great," I remarked. "Just great. *Now* look what you've done. This was what you *wanted*, wasn't it?"

"We meant to control it, Shawn," answered Chester. "We had calculated precise dosages for each person — exactly the amount that would activate a limited, specific range of responses to our suggestions."

"Everything was tested under stringent laboratory conditions," said Sylvester. "An overdose results in zombie-like obedience and wildly ridiculous behavior."

Screeching laughter echoed down the hall.

"How were we to know it would get out of hand?" Esther asked.

"Because . . . because you're not in a *lab*!" I shouted. "This is a *school*, with real-life kids! Or *was*. At this rate, we'll be closed by tomorrow."

"We were attempting to help," Sylvester said sadly.

"Some help." I stood up. "What planet are you guys from, anyway?"

With that, I stormed away.

Sylvester answered something, but I didn't hear it.

12

Chaos

"**W**atch ouuuuuuut!"

As I approached the front lobby, I was almost flattened. A big, hulking body hurtled around the corner.

"Yiiiii!" I screamed, jumping against the wall.

It was Mr. Dabney.

On Rollerblades.

"Waaa-hoooo!" he whooped, his pot belly jiggling from side to side.

I inched forward, close to the wall. The noise from the lobby was deafening.

Carefully I peeked around the corner. A football whizzed by my face. Spuds Dudigan, the HJHS team's wide receiver, made a leaping catch, sliding across the floor.

He knocked over a free-standing volleyball net. "Get off our court!" yelled one of the players.

I could not believe my eyes. The place was a zoo. Besides the volleyball game, and the football catch, some teachers were laying out bases for a softball game.

As Mr. Dabney barrelled in from another hallway, Waldo Wigglesworth held out a stopwatch and yelled, "World record, Dabney! Report to the office for your next assignment!"

"Hey, everybody! Look what we found!" Andrea Hyslop called out.

She and Mr. Reiley, the drama teacher, were pushing two racks from the HJHS costume shop.

"All riiiight!" Frank Mandolia bellowed.

The costumes were mobbed. Clothes flew into the air. Frank hopped away in a bunny getup. Trevor Van Pelt became a leprechaun. A ninth-grade girl named Sarah Bloom dressed in a long, flowing gown, strewing plastic flowers all around and singing, "Spring has sprung!"

Fred Bilecki went around wearing a toga and a plastic garland around his head, shouting, "Beware the idiots of March!"

Buford was on the floor, weeping with laughter.

In one hand, he held the end of a tape measure. At the other end, Mr. Asquith was carefully drawing a chalk mark on the floor.

I ran over to him. "What are you doing?" I demanded.

"What does it look like?" Buford shot back. "Measuring."

"For what?"

"A sand pit. For a tanning salon. See, you sit on a lounge chair and put these virtual reality glasses on, and — "

I was seeing red. I grabbed Buford by the lapel and slammed him against the wall.

"Are you too stupid to know what you're doing? Do you *want* our school to be torn down? Do you *want* us all to go to Pifflethorn next year? What if the state inspectors come?"

"Yo, lighten up, dude. It was going to happen anyway. Might as well have fun before it's too late. Besides, your geeky buds brought the food, not me."

"Oh, yeah? Well, this food was supposed to *save* the school. And it might have worked if you hadn't messed up the plan."

Buford chuckled. "Right. I'll believe that when monkeys fly out my nostrils. So what do you want *me* to do, huh? Why don't you ask the geeks to make an antelope?"

"Antidote!"

"Whatever."

"It's Friday. This is your last day at Hopnoodle. Couldn't you have just left us alone?"

"Ease up, Ferguson," Buford said. "In the long run, you'll thank me for this."

"Attention — hee hee hee — all students!" Mr. Dabney's voice echoed over the P.A. "In . . . oh, I don't know, I guess five or ten minutes or so — hoooooo hoo hoo! — we will have the skateboard race in the second floor east hallway. Or is it west? I don't know! Look for it! Haaaaaaah hah hah hah!"

Buford dropped the tape measure and bolted away. "You coming?" he asked.

Before I could answer, a Frisbee conked me on the head. I went to grab it and was hit in the chest with a spray of water.

With a loud giggle, Mr. Zoster waved his Super Soaker at me and shrugged. Next to him, Janice Taylor was doubled over, *cackling*.

Mrs. Glupe appeared, pushing a huge table with deep trays. "Make your own sundaes! Step right up!"

The stampede knocked me over.

I crawled away on my hands and knees. I had to get out of there. Call the police. Something.

Just then the front doors opened. Three men in construction clothes lumbered in. One of them cupped his hand over his mouth and shouted: "Okay, who called for the jackhammers?"

13

The Last Straw

"*Jackhammers?*" I shouted. "No! It's a mistake — "

Foosh!

Up skated Mr. Dabney.

Splat.

Down went Mr. Dabney.

"HAWWWWW haw haw haw haw!" he laughed. "Will you gentlemen help me up?"

One of the construction workers pulled him to his feet. "Who the heck are you?" he asked.

"I'm — hee hee — *the acting principal!* Can you believe it? HAAAAAAAAA!"

"Uh, we got a call for some emergency sidewalk removal?"

"Out front!" Mr. Dabney pointed. "The whole

darn thing! We need a hole for an Olympic-sized pool!"

"On the *lawn?*" one of the guys asked.

"No, *in the sky!*" Mr. Dabney clutched his stomach, convulsing with laughter.

"Yo, Dabney!" yelled Fred Bilecki from the office. "Get in here and play some tunes over the P.A."

"Excuse me, gentlemen," Mr. Dabney said, skating away.

Shaking their heads, the men left.

Through the glass doors, I could see two trucks parked at the curb, with the words *Fenster Contracting* painted on the side.

I ran out. Adam's dad was standing outside the truck, scratching his head. The three workers were unloading a jackhammer and setting it up.

"Mr. Fenster!" I called out. "Stop them."

"Shawn! What's going on in there?"

"It's — well, it's — " I stammered. "It's like temporary insanity."

"Ohhhhhh." Mr. Fenster nodded wisely. "I heard about something like this once . . . some germ got into the heating ducts, made people act all weird?"

"Uh, yeah, something like that!"

Mr. Fenster chuckled. "Good thing Adam's

home sick today," he said. "Okay, boys, start at the far end."

"What are you doing?" I blurted. "Mr. Dabney didn't mean it! He's not in his right mind!"

Mr. Fenster shrugged. "Hey, we have a contract, we do the work. If they want to put it all back, we can do that, too."

"But you can't!"

"Talk to Dabney."

I raced back inside. Loud rock music was now booming over the P.A.

Crassshhhh! The trophy case exploded in a shower of glass. I hit the floor.

"Home run!" someone yelled.

"No way! Ground rules double!"

This was totally out of hand. I stood up and shouted, *"Hey! Everybody knock it off!"*

Splurshh!

I didn't see the cherry pie until it hit me in the face.

When I scraped the glop away from my eyes, I could see Mrs. Glupe and Sarah Bloom doubled over, red-faced from giggling.

"Yeeahhh, rock on!" Mr. Dabney's voice rang out. "This is WHJHS, Radio Hopnoodle, and I'm DJ Jazzy Dabney, playing requests until we drop! But first these announcements: A seminar on

Home Video Making is being held right now in room 204. Mr. Armstrong is conducting Frisbee Technique in the gym, to be followed by Trends in Baseball Capwear . . . and now, more music!"

I flung a hunk of cherry pie away.

"Yeeow!"

I spun around. Lianna Walker was wiping the pie off her face with a paper towel.

"Oh! Sorry!" I said.

She held out a roll of paper towels to me. "Here. I borrowed these from the boys' room. Don't tell anyone."

"Thanks." I cleaned myself off. Lianna was soaking wet.

"I got doused by Mr. Zoster," she said. "Shawn, I'm . . . so sorry about all this."

"*You're* sorry?"

She nodded. "I was sitting next to Sylvester on the bus. I saw what happened to Adam. If only I'd *done* something. . . ."

"Lianna, it's not your fault. It's out of our control."

(*That* was an understatement.)

"Isn't there anything we can do?"

I swallowed hard.

With her deep brown eyes, Lianna seemed to be penetrating to the depths of my soul. I was a captive to her wishes. I had to obey. For the sake of the school. For the sake of Hopnoodle.

For the sake of Lianna.

I wiped off the last bits of pie. My mind was racing. I had to command the teachers — all the teachers — to stop. Isolate them, the way I had isolated Adam.

"Yeeeeee-hah!" Mr. Dabney's voice blared. "And now for some heavy metalllll!"

"The mike!" I exclaimed.

"Mike? Mike who?" Lianna asked.

"Mr. Dabney's microphone! That's how we can control the teachers! We can order them around, all at once!"

We took off toward the office.

But the moment we saw the front door, we froze.

Mr. Petard was walking into the school. Behind him were a man and a woman in business suits. Their eyes were as wide as baseballs.

A small chunk of plaster fell from the ceiling and landed on Mr. Petard's head.

"Who — wha — " Mr. Petard sputtered.

I ran to the office door. "Mr. Dabney!"

Whoosh! Out he skated, giggling. "Heyyyyy, Horst, babycakes! What's up?"

"What is the *meaning* of this?" Mr. Petard demanded.

"Beats me, boss! Heeeeeee hee hee! Hey, who are the suits?"

"Uh, these are Ms. Stumpf and Mr. Trezza from the state inspection board — "

"Welcome," Mr. Dabney said. "Cool place, huh?"

The woman — Ms. Stumpf — turned to Mr. Petard with a scowl. "I think we've seen enough, Mr. Petard. Have it torn down as soon as you can!"

14

The Aftermath

P^{*link!*}
   I kicked a piece of broken glass against the wall. Mr. Trumple was dancing with a broom, more or less sweeping up the debris in the empty lobby.

The floor rumbled from the vibrations of the jackhammers outside. Nobody had bothered telling the workers the school was condemned.

I sighed. As I wandered around the hallways, my footsteps echoed dully. It was three o'clock. Trevor Van Pelt had commanded Mr. Dabney to dismiss the school early.

It being a Friday, no one had complained.

Lianna had stuck around awhile, too, but she was too depressed to stay.

Me? I didn't really want to go home. I knew I'd

have to answer a million questions once the news got out. And how could I explain *this*?

I walked past the cafeteria. All the teachers and staff were sacked out on the benches, snoring away. They looked like little kids at naptime.

Only not as cute.

I guess sleepiness was another side effect of the candy. Either that, or the grown-ups just didn't have what it took to act like kids.

Funny, they really seemed to have enjoyed goofing off.

On the wall, someone had written *Hopnoodle Rules!* in hot fudge sauce.

I picked up a rubber fright mask off the floor and used it to smudge the words so they looked like a big blob. Then I took the mask and flung it as far as I could.

I didn't care where it landed. What was the difference? The whole place was going to be torn down anyway.

And what was going to happen to us in the meantime? Were we all supposed to squeeze into the Pifflethorn classes until the addition was built? Maybe we'd all have to stand in the back. Sit on the floor. Or outside in the snow.

I felt so weird. I wanted to scream, but I also wanted to cry and laugh and bash my head against the wall.

I thought and thought about which to do, but I couldn't decide. When I reached the back of the school, I stared through a window across the athletic field.

The old Hopnoodle Ooga Horn factory, dark with soot, loomed over the field. I hadn't seen Sylvester, Chester, or Esther since the whole mess began. Maybe they'd all run back there, to figure out some other mutant formula with their dad.

"Too late now," I said under my breath.

"Ohhhhhh . . ."

I turned with a start.

"Hello!" I called. "Who's there?"

"Ohhhhhh . . ."

The moan was coming from an open door — the stage door to the auditorium. A foot was sticking out of it.

I ran to it and looked inside.

"*Shawwwwwwn . . .*" a voice groaned.

The breath caught in my throat.

Sylvester was sprawled on his back. His skin was blue and shriveled, his hair silver and cobwebby. He reached up toward me. "Helllp . . . us."

Us?

I looked past him. Chester had collapsed in a heap backstage. Wisps of smoke curled up around him.

On the other side of the stage, Esther was crawling to a bank of lighting equipment. She had a wire hanger in her hand.

"Esther!" I called out.

She cast a weak glance over her shoulder. Her eyes were hollow and sad.

Then she turned and inserted the hanger in an electric socket.

15

Shocking Events

*D*ZZZZZZT!
Bright sparks engulfed Esther. She shook uncontrollably. I had to shield my eyes.

"*No-o-o-o-o-o!*" The word tore out of my throat. I ran blindly across the stage, tripping over ropes and wires.

I tumbled to the ground and rolled.

When I stopped, I was looking up at Esther.

"Greetings!" she said with a big grin.

The green had returned to her hair. Her braces shone brilliantly.

I pointed to the socket. "But — but you — you — "

Without answering, Esther ran to Chester and started dragging him toward the lighting board. "Help me, Shawn," she said.

I uncoiled myself. Numbly I grabbed Chester's ankle and helped drag him.

Esther curled his fingers around the wire hanger. I ran behind a half-closed curtain and cringed.

DZZZZZZT!

When I peeked around the curtain, Chester was hugging his sister with a huge smile. Together, they glowed.

Literally.

They didn't need me to drag over Sylvester, and I didn't volunteer.

But I watched this time.

Sylvester shook as the electricity shot through him. The lights in the auditorium dimmed and almost went out. Sylvester was lit as bright as Fourth of July fireworks.

When he let go, the lights popped back to full strength and Sylvester let out a huge burp.

"Excuse me," he said, "but that was awfully tasty."

I staggered forward. My legs didn't seem to want to work. "Uh . . . uh . . . uh . . ." I said.

"Would you like some, Shawn?" Chester asked.

"*NO!*" My voice was a high-pitched hysterical squeak. "What are you — what hap — why . . . WHAT *ARE* YOU?"

The Ghieks all looked at each other. "Perhaps we had better sit," Sylvester said.

I dropped to the floor.

Sylvester, Esther, and Chester sat calmly in front of me.

"You're . . . not from this neighborhood, are you?" I asked.

"Oh, yes indeed, we are," Esther said.

Sylvester chuckled. "It's too much of a hassle to travel outside the Milky Way."

"The Milky — very funny. I get it."

The three Ghieks stared blankly at me.

"Okay, *not* funny," I said quickly. "Go on."

Esther took a deep breath. "Well, we come from Herpnodl X. It's in a cozy little cluster near what you call Orion's belt — "

"*Herpnodl?*" I interrupted.

The three of them smiled. "Yes, you can see we had sentimental reasons for choosing your village," Esther said.

"All the other names were so ugly," Chester added.

"Anyway, for eons we Herpnodlians were ignorant of our planet's ecology," Esther said. "We wasted our food source."

"What you call electricity," Sylvester explained.

"You *eat* electricity?" I asked.

"In a manner of speaking," Esther replied. "Anyway, you've seen what happens to us when we do not have enough."

"We harnessed our sun's power but thought little of conservation," Chester said. "Now it is dimming dangerously."

"We were sent on a mission to find alternate fuel sources," Sylvester went on. "And your planet seemed to have an interesting one."

"Food," I said.

"Yes," Chester agreed. "We have some similar sources on Herpnodl, also. So we thought we'd investigate in hopes we could adapt ourselves to matter-ingestion."

"We studied your people quite closely." Sylvester nervously patted his green hair. "Of course, we did not achieve accuracy on everything."

"Why the name Ghieks?" I asked.

"We wanted to name ourselves after the most admirable people in your history," Esther said.

"*Geeks?*"

She shook her head. "Ancient Greeks. The registrar at the Galactic Name Bureau made a mistake copying it down. How did you become Shawn Ferguson?"

"I was named after my German great-grandfather."

"Also Shawn Ferguson?" Sylvester asked.

"No, Johannes Sicherheit," I replied. "His American relatives told him to shorten his name to John Heit. But he was so tired when he got to this country that when the immigration guy asked his name, he said, 'I Forgot' in German. *'Schon Vergessen.'* "

"I do not follow," Esther said.

"The guy wrote 'Shawn Ferguson.' That's how *he* heard it. You know, sort of like 'Ghiek' only not so bad."

Sylvester smiled. "So we have something in common, my friend."

"Yeah, I guess."

Esther must have known what was on my mind. She put her hand on my shoulder and said, "Shawn, we are terribly sorry for the pain we caused. Our papa, as you might guess, is experimenting night and day with the chemical properties of your food. We . . ." She cast a guilty look at her brothers. "We wanted so badly to help you, we took this particular batch from him while he was not looking."

Chester sighed. "When he finds out, he will ground us."

"Yeah. Well." I stood up. "I guess we all make mistakes, huh?"

As I began walking toward the door, Esther

called out, "Shawn, wait. We will see our father shortly. Tonight we all must attend the welcoming ceremony for Ghiek Industries in Town Hall. Will you be there?"

I shrugged. "I don't know."

"I recommend you go," Esther said.

"Why should I?" I asked.

Esther smiled. "We may be able to make some sparks fly."

16

Hoodwinked

" **A**nd by the power vested in me as mayor of
this great village, I hereby officially welcome
Ghiek Industries to Hopnoodle!" Mayor Glipnik
announced.

The audience clapped politely. A lot of people
had shown. Practically the whole village. I
couldn't find the Fensters, though, so I was a little
worried. I hadn't called Adam since I'd arrived
home from school. I hoped he was okay.

From the side of the stage, an old man with a
green-tinged beard approached the podium on
rickety legs. Behind him were Sylvester, Esther,
and Chester.

The old man looked as if he wanted to take the

mike, but Mayor Glipnik stepped right in front of him. "Mr. Ghiek, we cannot *tell* you how tre*men*-dously *proud* we are — "

I felt a tug on my sleeve.

"Shawn!"

It was Lianna. A frog leaped into my throat. "Uh . . . hey, what's up?"

Her eyes were full of urgency. She brought her face close to mine. She was breathing heavily. Her lips began to part. I almost passed out.

But she pushed my face to the side and whispered in my ear, *"The school! They're tearing it down!"*

"I know!" I whispered back. *"I saw the inspectors. Remember?"*

"No! I mean now!"

Outside, I could hear the rumbling of trucks. To the left of the stage, Mr. Petard was nervously looking at his watch.

"Come on, Shawn!" Lianna pulled me by the arm. I grabbed my coat and we ran outside.

Two *Fenster Contracting* dump trucks were making the right turn at the end of the block, heading toward Hopnoodle Junior High.

"But — so soon?" I said.

"Petard is pulling a fast one!" Lianna's breath made little clouds in the bleak late-winter night air. "He's a crook, Shawn. He knows he's about to be sued for the land, and he wants those condos up before the court takes away his building permit. He figured he could sneak the wreckers in while everyone was at the meeting."

"How do you *know* this?"

"On my way home from school, I stopped in at Adam's. I felt bad about what had happened to him this morning. Anyway, while I was there, Adam's mom took the call from Petard. She had to page Mr. Fenster at school, because he was still ripping up the sidewalk."

Of course. That's why the Fensters hadn't shown up. Mr. Fenster was doing Petard's dirty work.

My mind was racing. "I've got to call Adam."

"I'm going back into the meeting to tell all the kids I can find." She reached into her jeans pocket and took out a fistful of quarters. "You saw who was in there. Call everyone who wasn't. I want as many kids at the school as possible. Now."

"Right."

I took the quarters. Lianna ran inside the village hall. Quickly I punched Adam's number.

"Hello?"

"Adam?"

"Shawn?"

"Adam . . . listen closely. After I hang up, pick up the phone and page your father. Tell him, 'Stop the trucks!' Do you understand, Adam?"

"Will you cut the Frankenstein business?" Adam said. "I have a splitting headache."

"You mean . . . you're *normal?*"

"I wouldn't go that far."

"Esther said it was supposed to last twenty-four hours."

"Guess that's why she's a geek and we're not."

"Listen, Adam, did Lianna talk to you?"

"No. Mom said she started looking sick and ran out."

"Well, your dad has been hired to tear down the school. Now."

"What?"

"Meet me there!"

I hung up. One by one, I called all the kids whose numbers I knew by heart. Then I called information for the others.

In about ten minutes, Lianna was walking out of the meeting with a dozen kids in down coats. "Let's go!" she said.

We ran the entire mile to the school. As we approached, I could see the top of a crane peeking over the trees.

I sprinted ahead. An enormous black metal ball hung from the crane, swinging slowly back and forth. Inside the crane, a worker was swiveling the ball closer to the school. Mr. Fenster stood a few feet away, holding a walkie-talkie.

"Okay," I heard him shout. "Let 'er rip!"

17

The Wrecker's Ball, the Human Wall

"Stop!" I called out.

Mr. Fenster shot a glance over his shoulder. His eyes widened. "Hold it, Josh!" he shouted into the walkie-talkie.

The ball was swinging now, just missing the school's brick wall.

I ran to the front door.

"Shawn!" Mr. Fenster shouted. "Are you crazy? What the heck are you doing?"

Lianna ran up beside me. She grabbed my hand. Together we faced the wrecker.

The ball was to our left, its swing gradually narrowing.

Our friends were gathered at the curb, about thirty strong. Nobody was moving.

Mr. Fenster stormed toward us, the veins in his forehead bulging. "Get away from there! You're going to get yourselves killed! We have a *job* to do!"

He reached out to grab me by the collar. But before he could, Frank Mandolia stepped forward and took Lianna's hand.

Andrea Hyslop followed and took *his* hand.

Then Trevor Van Pelt.

Then Sarah Bloom. And Fred Bilecki, and Janice Taylor, and Spuds Dudigan.

One at a time, then all together, the entire crowd moved to the front door and stayed there, holding hands. We stood across the front of the school like a wall.

Then, panting up the street, totally out of breath, ran Adam.

"*Adam, you go right home!*" Mr. Fenster thundered.

But Adam went to the end of the line and held on tight, his breaths heaving loudly.

"Aw, come on — how can we — " Mr. Fenster threw up his hands. "*Kiiiids!*"

"This is illegal, Mr. Fenster," I began.

SCREEEEEEEEEEE!

A shiny black Mercedes squealed to a stop at

the curb. The driver's door opened and Mr. Petard bustled out.

"Fenster!" he roared. "What's going on here?"

Mr. Fenster shook his head. "They just showed up, Mr. Petard. And they won't move."

Mr. Petard stood inches away from him, glaring eyeball to eyeball. "Well, of *course* they won't!" he roared. "This is their school! The place where they've met! Grown up! Learned and laughed together!"

"Well, yes, I know, sir, but you said — "

"Never mind what I said, Mr. Fenster! What kind of a society is it where a thinking adult can't listen to a committed group of its young people?" Mr. Petard walked toward us with a warm, confident smile. "I *like* your fighting spirit, kids. *I* was like that at your age."

"Don't knock down our school, Mr. Petard," I said. "It's not right."

Lianna squeezed my hand tighter. Sweat was forming all across my scalp.

"That's precisely the point, isn't it? Doing the *right* thing. I — I guess I'd been temporarily blinded by my zeal for the good of Hopnoodle." Mr. Petard sighed deeply. "Now, standing here, seeing your protest, I am profoundly affected. I want to hear your side of the story, kids. To talk things out before acting. In a spirit of cooperation." He held out his hands. "What do you say?"

I looked at Lianna. She nodded and turned back to Mr. Petard. "Okay, let's talk."

"Come over by my car," Mr. Petard said. "I don't want you standing so near this crane. I'd never forgive myself if an accident happened."

Everyone in the line was looking at me now. Mr. Petard was right about the crane. If it tipped, or if a sharp wind caught that ball, it could be dangerous. "All right," I said. "Let's go, everybody."

Slowly we peeled away from the entrance. Mr. Petard walked quickly to his car, and we followed close behind.

Workers stepped out of the trucks and watched us. They lined up between us and the school, holding their tools and waiting.

As we gathered around Mr. Petard, he asked Lianna, "So, who's your ringleader? You, young woman?"

"And Shawn," Lianna said.

Mr. Petard smiled. Then his eyes seemed to fix on something behind her. For a moment they grew cold.

He nodded.

"Okay, *go!*" shouted Mr. Fenster into his walkie-talkie.

I turned around. The workers were shoulder-to-shoulder, holding sledgehammers and crowbars, facing us defiantly.

And the metal ball began swinging once again.

We had been tricked!

18

The Right Thing

*P*HWEEEEEEEEEEEET!
A loud whistle broke the silence, along with the puttering of an old engine.

A Weiner's Wieners truck swooped up to the curb.

"Break time!" shouted a voice from inside.

The workers dropped their tools. Josh, the crane operator, hopped out. Clapping each other on the back, the men ambled over to the truck.

Mr. Petard looked as if he were about to explode. *"What are you doing, you fools?"*

Mr. Fenster shrugged and pointed to his watch. "Union rules."

I watched in amazement. How could Dad know . . . ?

But it wasn't Dad. It was another Weiner's Wie-

101

ners guy. He had a silver-gray beard, but it was hard to see his face. Instead of a rubber wiener cap, he wore a wide-brimmed felt hat.

"Quick, Shawn," Lianna said. "Let's do something!"

"Come on, everybody! Form the wall!" Taking Lianna's hand, I ran toward the school.

But now the workers were running, too. Racing. Laughing all the way. One of them threw a hot dog in the air and caught it in his mouth.

They got to the front door before we did. They pulled it open and ran inside.

We crammed in front, looking through the glass doors.

Lianna quickly looked back at the truck. When she turned around again, she was grinning.

Pulling open the door, she yelled into the school at the top of her lungs: *"Partyyyy!"*

One of the workers picked up a Frisbee. "Yo, Ralphie!" he called out. "Catch!"

As Ralphie went running, he stepped on a piece of cherry pie and slipped. "Who-o-o-o-oa!" He hit the ground, howling with laughter.

Another worker whizzed by him on a skateboard.

Still another had taken a Toxic Avenger mask from the costume rack and was running around the lobby, grunting.

Two pairs of guys were chicken-fighting near the principal's office.

"Stop them!" Mr. Petard commanded.

I looked back. He was standing by the curb, in total shock.

By the Weiner's Wieners truck, the driver smiled and took off his hat to us.

Under it was a thin, tufted mass of gray-green hair.

"Lester!" Mr. Petard shouted. "You traitor!"

"It's Mr. Ghiek!" I blurted out.

"I'm heading back to the village hall!" Mr. Ghiek called to us. "I can take a couple of you with me!"

Lianna and I jumped into the cab.

"We'll run there, right behind you!" Adam shouted.

Vrooooom!

The Mercedes engine started up. I could see the whites of Mr. Petard's eyes through his windshield.

Mr. Ghiek stepped on the gas. We took off, winding through the streets of Hopnoodle Village.

When we arrived at the village hall, I jumped out.

With a screech of tires, the Mercedes hopped the curb, drove onto the sidewalk, and cut me off.

Mr. Petard jumped out. "Where do you think you're going?" he said to me.

"To do the right thing, Mr. Petard," I replied. "Just like you said."

Lianna and Mr. Ghiek emerged from the truck. "Turncoat!" Mr. Petard said to the old man. "You fed those workers tainted food. I can have you arrested."

"We'll see who's arrested first," I said, running around the Mercedes.

Mr. Petard bolted after me. As I pulled on the door, I felt him grabbing my collar.

"Hey — "

I was choking. Lianna and Mr. Ghiek were trying to pull him away. The auditorium was down a long hallway, and it would take a loud yell for someone to hear.

I opened my mouth, but no sound came out except gagging noises. I was starting to feel weak.

I let go of the door and it swung closed.

Red stars formed before my eyes. Behind me, all the grunting and scuffling was fading in my ears. Everything started becoming darker and darker.

Slowly I sank to the ground.

19

Lester to the Rescue

The door burst open.

Mr. Petard let go and I fell.

"Heyyyyy, Mr. Petard! It certainly is nice to see you!"

My vision was clearing again. Enough to see Buford's disgusting face looming above me.

"Uh . . . ahem, you're the . . . uh, Tutweiler boy, is that right?" Mr. Petard said.

"What an uncanny memory! Yes, as a matter of fact, I am." Buford stepped around me as if I *always* spent time on the floor. "Uh, hello, Shawn. Lianna. Anyway, Mr. Petard, I came here tonight just to tell you about a great idea I have to benefit the kids of Pifflethorn Middle School — "

"Er, but — excuse me — " Mr. Petard protested.

Buford backed him against the wall. "I'm concerned with the teaching of economics, Mr. Petard — which brings me to the topic of paper towel distribution in the school's new addition — "

I scrambled to my feet and ran inside.

Sylvester, Chester, and Esther were still onstage, and Mayor Glipnik was still speaking. "And so, whereas we shall soon be the proud beneficiaries of a new industry, leading to unprecedented economic growth, I hereby declare this to be . . . Ghiek Week!"

"Just a minute!" I called out. "Stop the meeting!"

I ran past rows of half-sleeping listeners. Leaping onto the stage, I grabbed the mike.

"Goodness," Mayor Glipnik said. "This was not scheduled — "

"Everybody, listen up!" I said into the mike. "While you've been sitting here, Mr. Petard has sent wreckers to tear down Hopnoodle Junior High!"

Mr. Petard burst through the door. "Stop him!"

"He's trying to get it done before he's arrested!" I said.

"It's a lie!" Mr. Petard yelled, lumbering down the aisle.

The audience sprang to life. My dad stood up and shouted, "Let him speak!"

"Yeah!" a couple of other voices agreed.

"Go for it," Esther's voice urged from behind me.

"It's not fair!" I announced. "We need our school. Mr. Petard is interested in making money for *himself*!"

"Does he have a permit for demolition?" someone asked.

"I don't know, but — "

Mr. Petard leaped onto the stage and grabbed the mike. "Ladies and gentlemen, no need to be alarmed," he said. "The workers at the school are merely, er, taking measurements. I assure you that all legal avenues are being followed, and Hopnoodle's greater interests will be served."

"Heck, I don't care if you are knocking the place down tonight!" shouted one parent. "I'm no fool. I *want* my child in Pifflethorn next year!"

Left and right, voices called out, "Yeah!" and "That's right!" and "You tell 'im!" and "Ignorant yokel!" and "Let the kid speak!"

Parents began calling names. Screaming. It was pure pandemonium.

"Order! Order!" Mayor Glipnik pounded his gavel on the podium, but it was no use.

By now Lianna and Mr. Ghiek were onstage beside me. I turned to the old man and whispered, "I *know* who you are! You're just *using* us. You don't mean to stay here forever. What's going to happen to us when you leave?"

Mr. Ghiek looked directly into my eyes. I couldn't tell what he was feeling. "My children and I have caused much controversy," was all he said.

"Go up there!" Lianna pleaded with him. "Tell them you'll . . . move your company to another town if they do this!"

But Mr. Ghiek looked past us to the podium.

At the other end of the stage, my dad was climbing the stairs. He took the mike from Mr. Petard and said, "*I* went to Hopnoodle Junior High, ladies and gentlemen! So did my father and mother, and their fathers and mothers. As did many of yours. Sure the building's too old and too small — but it's full of memories. And if we lose those, we lose a little bit of ourselves. I say, forget the condos — turn the building into a recreation center and build a new school on the land next to it!"

A roar of approval went up.

"Over my dead body!" thundered Mr. Petard. "I *own* that land and — "

"How about using the factory?"

Mr. Ghiek's voice was high-pitched and piercing. Everyone shut up.

He waddled over to the podium. With a friendly smile, he took the mike from my dad. "Mr. Petard does not own my factory," he said. "*I* do. And I must announce, due to unforeseen circumstances, I must relocate my business."

Everyone began murmuring at once.

A sudden noise drew my eyes to the back of the auditorium. Adam was pushing open the doors, leading in the kids who had run all the way from school. Buford was with them, looking totally dumbfounded.

"Uh . . . oh, my!" Mayor Glipnik said. "Sshh! Order! Order!"

"Now, my building is large, solidly built, and well-lit," Mr. Ghiek continued. "According to the federal official I contacted, the building would be eligible for a large renovation grant — *if* I turned it over to public use. So I will bequeath it to the village of Hopnoodle, under the condition that you convert it into a new, state-of-the-art middle school!"

"YEEEEAAAAAAHHHHH!" The shout from the back of the auditorium was deafening.

Mayor Glipnik pounded his gavel again. "*Please!*"

"And then, afterward," Mr. Ghiek announced, "my children and I will travel to another planet in another solar system, where ingestion of rock material is the primary source of food."

Total, stunned silence.

My stomach sank.

"We have enjoyed the energy of your people, and your convenient sources of electricity, and we have made some advances in our genetic studies, but we are causing too much trouble here, and as I always say . . ." He chuckled. "There's no place like Herpnodl. Not even Hopnoodle."

Sylvester rose to put a hand on his father's shoulder. Chester and Esther ran up and gave him a hug.

"What is he talking about?" I heard someone whisper.

"It's a joke, right?" someone else asked.

"He's a crackpot!" an old woman shouted.

"Look at the hair!"

"They're mutants!"

"Geeks!"

"GEEEEEEEEEKS!"

I buried my face in my hands.

Epilogue

Well, now you know the real story of the geeks.

The rest, of course, you've heard on the news. Well, sort of. They missed a few things, as you can imagine.

They told you that Mr. Petard was arrested the next day for demolition without a permit, plus all kinds of real estate and tax stuff I couldn't begin to understand. They covered his trial and showed a video of his walk to jail, where he'll serve ten to fifteen with no parole (the black eye and split lip were given to him by Ms. Stritch when she returned).

And they covered Pifflethorn's great recession, after Mr. Petard went bankrupt.

They also reported how the old Hopnoodle Junior High was turned into a great rec center with indoor-outdoor pools. And how the Hopnoodle Ooga Horn/Ghiek Industries factory became Hopnoodle Middle School. *And* how Fenster Contracting won national awards for renovation and became Fensterworks International, Ltd. (You probably remember seeing Adam riding a horse across the lawn of Mr. Petard's thirty-seven-room mansion, which Mr. Fenster bought and fixed up for his family.)

But they *didn't* tell you that my dad became the president of the rec center and the new mayor of Hopnoodle Village. Or that he gave over his Weiner's Wieners truck to Beauregard Tutweiler, Buford's father. (Buford didn't mind. He sits in the passenger seat whenever he can, with a roll of paper towels, now seven cents a sheet.)

They also didn't tell you that Lianna Walker and I actually went on a date. That's right. Unfortunately, the movie was PG-13 and the ticket people were strict, so she went in alone and we haven't seen each other since.

Oh, well, I'll be thirteen soon, and there's always hope.

Anyway, the most important thing they never told you was what happened to the Ghieks.

That Saturday night, as all this stuff was happening, I found a box of chocolates, addressed to me, on our doorstep. The Newt had already ripped the brown paper off, but I grabbed the box out of his hands. (Which was fine. He loves to eat brown paper.)

I raced up to my room. Jumping onto my bed, I opened it. Inside, on top of the wax paper, was a small white envelope.

I pulled out a note and read:

My dear Shawn,
If this is what food does to living organisms,
We'll stick with electricity as long as we can.
Thank you for a thrilling ride.

♡ Love,
Esther

I sighed. Already I was missing the Ghieks.

I popped a caramel into my mouth, then a coconut cream. Outside my window, a late-winter snow had begun to fall. It blanketed the street and made everything so silent.

The sky was a flat gray-black. It was as if the stars had emptied from it and fallen to the earth as snowflakes.

Snow. That was Dad's description of the stars,

back when we were in the truck and he told me his tall story about the Leap Year Lights.

I smiled. It seemed like eons ago.

Time for another chocolate.

Just before I looked down, I thought I spotted a flash of green. Just over the ridge of trees beyond our block.

A low, whirring noise began.

I pressed my face to the window. In the distance, a glowing disk rose into the air. It hovered for a moment, then swooped toward my house.

I backed away. A piece of coconut got stuck in my throat and I coughed.

The green disk seemed to grow larger as it approached. It revolved slowly, until I could see a long window.

Inside, I made out three silhouettes, each with a spiky mass of hair. Together, they waved.

Then, with a sudden whoosh, the disk was gone.

I looked at my chocolates and panicked. They were from Esther! What if —

Behind me, my door opened. Dad walked in and tripped over a pile of clothes.

"Uh, Shawn," he said sternly, "Nathaniel says that — "

"Dad," I interrupted. "Tell me to clean up my room."

"Look, young man, you know I shouldn't have to *tell* you — "

"No, Dad, just *do* it. Say the words."

"Er, all right." He cleared his throat. "Clean up your room, Shawn."

"*No!*" I replied happily, of my own free will. "No way!"

I burst out laughing.

Dad just stared at me as if I'd lost my mind.

"Here, Dad," I said. "Have a chocolate."

About the Author

Peter Lerangis started writing stories during elementary school math, in spiral notebooks hidden inside his textbook. (Despite this, he claims to have done well in math, although no records can be found to confirm that.) He grew up in Freeport, New York, and was graduated from Harvard College. Before he became a writer, he was an actor and singer. Nowadays he lives in New York City with his wife and two sons, a stone's throw from Central Park.

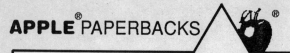

APPLE® PAPERBACKS

Pick an Apple and Polish Off Some Great Reading!

BEST-SELLING APPLE TITLES

❏ MT43944-8	**Afternoon of the Elves** Janet Taylor Lisle	**$2.75**
❏ MT43109-9	**Boys Are Yucko** Anna Grossnickle Hines	**$2.95**
❏ MT43473-X	**The Broccoli Tapes** Jan Slepian	**$2.95**
❏ MT40961-1	**Chocolate Covered Ants** Stephen Manes	**$2.95**
❏ MT45436-6	**Cousins** Virginia Hamilton	**$2.95**
❏ MT44036-5	**George Washington's Socks** Elvira Woodruff	**$2.95**
❏ MT45244-4	**Ghost Cadet** Elaine Marie Alphin	**$2.95**
❏ MT44351-8	**Help! I'm a Prisoner in the Library** Eth Clifford	**$2.95**
❏ MT43618-X	**Me and Katie (The Pest)** Ann M. Martin	**$2.95**
❏ MT43030-0	**Shoebag** Mary James	**$2.95**
❏ MT46075-7	**Sixth Grade Secrets** Louis Sachar	**$2.95**
❏ MT42882-9	**Sixth Grade Sleepover** Eve Bunting	**$2.95**
❏ MT41732-0	**Too Many Murphys** Colleen O'Shaughnessy McKenna	**$2.95**

Available wherever you buy books, or use this order form.

- -

Scholastic Inc., P.O. Box 7502, 2931 East McCarty Street, Jefferson City, MO 65102

Please send me the books I have checked above. I am enclosing $_____ (please add $2.00 to cover shipping and handling). Send check or money order — no cash or C.O.D.s please.

Name_____ **Birthdate**_____

Address _____

City_____ **State/Zip** _____

Please allow four to six weeks for delivery. Offer good in the U.S.A. only. Sorry, mail orders are not available to residents of Canada. Prices subject to change.

APP693

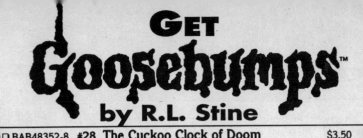

GET Goosebumps™
by R.L. Stine

☐ BAB48352-8	#28	The Cuckoo Clock of Doom	$3.50
☐ BAB48351-X	#27	A Night in Terror Tower	$3.50
☐ BAB48350-1	#26	My Hairiest Adventure	$3.50
☐ BAB48355-2	#25	Attack of the Mutant	$3.25
☐ BAB48354-4	#24	Phantom of the Auditorium	$3.25
☐ BAB47745-5	#23	Return of the Mummy	$3.25
☐ BAB47744-7	#22	Ghost Beach	$3.25
☐ BAB47743-9	#21	Go Eat Worms!	$3.25
☐ BAB47742-0	#20	The Scarecrow Walks at Midnight	$3.25
☐ BAB47741-2	#19	Deep Trouble	$3.25
☐ BAB47740-4	#18	Monster Blood II	$3.25
☐ BAB47739-0	#17	Why I'm Afraid of Bees	$3.25
☐ BAB47738-2	#16	One Day at Horrorland	$3.25
☐ BAB49450-3	#15	You Can't Scare Me!	$3.25
☐ BAB49449-X	#14	The Werewolf of Fever Swamp	$3.25
☐ BAB49448-1	#13	Piano Lessons Can Be Murder	$3.25
☐ BAB49447-3	#12	Be Careful What You Wish For...	$3.25
☐ BAB49446-5	#11	The Haunted Mask	$3.25
☐ BAB49445-7	#10	The Ghost Next Door	$3.25
☐ BAB46619-4	#9	Welcome to Camp Nightmare	$3.25
☐ BAB46618-6	#8	The Girl Who Cried Monster	$3.25
☐ BAB46617-8	#7	Night of the Living Dummy	$3.25
☐ BAB45370-X	#6	Let's Get Invisible!	$3.25
☐ BAB45369-6	#5	The Curse of the Mummy's Tomb	$3.25
☐ BAB45368-8	#4	Say Cheese and Die!	$3.25
☐ BAB45367-X	#3	Monster Blood	$3.25
☐ BAB45366-1	#2	Stay Out of the Basement	$3.25
☐ BAB45365-3	#1	Welcome to Dead House	$3.25

Scare me, thrill me, mail me GOOSEBUMPS Now!